For my sister, Angela

A.M.L.

Woo!
Written and illustrated by Ana Martín Larrañaga
British Library Cataloguing in Publication Data
A catalogue record of this book is available from the British Library
ISBN 0 340 77405 3 (HB)
ISBN 0 340 77406 1 (PB)
Copyright © Ana Martín Larrañaga 2000

First edition published 2000
10 9 8 7 6 5 4 3 2 1

Published by Hodder Children's Books
a division of Hodder Headline,
338 Euston Road, London NW1 3BH
Printed in Hong Kong

Woo!

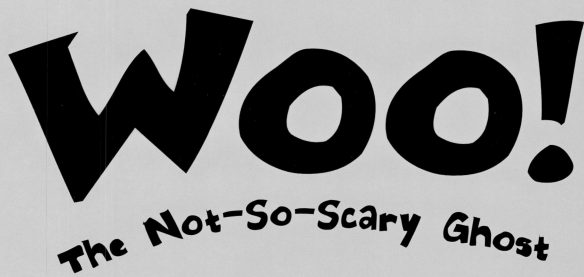

The Not-So-Scary Ghost

By

Ana Martín Larrañaga

Hodder
Children's
Books

A division of Hodder Headline

Woo wishes he were big and scary.
He is fed up with everyone
telling him what to do.

Brush your teeth . . .

Do your homework . . .

Feed the cat . . .

Tidy your room . . .

So, in the dark just before dawn, when all good little ghosts have kissed their mummies and daddies good morning and gone to bed . . .

. . . Woo packs his bag and flits away,
out of the window.

Woo has fun practising his scaring techniques . . .

. . . although nothing quite works.

Then, as the sun comes up,
Woo gets more scared than scary.

Little ghosts shouldn't be out all by themselves
in the daytime . . . but where can he hide?

The dog isn't scared of Woo,
he just doesn't like visitors . . .

... and the farmer doesn't like the dog playing with her clean sheets.

Poor Woo! Things are getting worse . . .

. . . and worse and worse.

The goat wants to eat him.
The dog wants to chase him.

The kittens want to play with him.
And the farmer wants . . .

...to squash him! Then...

riiing

riiing

There is only one thing standing
between Woo and his big escape . . .

Woooo!

shouts Woo.

Woo makes it home just in time,
as the sun and moon are changing places.

Just in time for kisses good night
and pancakes before school.

Even scary ghosts
love home sweet
home, thinks Woo.

Where's my sheet?
thinks the farmer.